LAND ACKNOWLEDGMENT

Sift was written on the land of Cayuse, Umatilla, Walla Walla, Kalapuya, Atfalati, Ahantchuyuk, and the Confederated Tribes of Grand Ronde and of Siletz Indians.

And The 3rd Thing is located at the southern tip of the Salish Sea on the traditional, unceded land of the Medicine Creek Treaty Tribes, among them, the Nisqually, Squaxin and Stehchass peoples. As part of our work to create a culture of intimacy, accountability and radical imagination, we acknowledge the legacy and ongoing violence of colonial settlement and commit to cultivating restorative relationships with Indigenous communities and with the land.

In support of truth-telling and reconciliation, and with the belief that a book can be a liberated and liberatory space that travels through time and across borders, each project of our 2023 Cohort shares space with Indigenous poet Abigail Chabitnoy. We are honored to offer excerpts from her ongoing work "DISQUIET ARK." Petitionary and stark, its darkly glimmering shards cut openings through which we might pass into an intimate eternity.

ABIGAIL CHABITNOY

Abigail Chabitnoy is a Koniag descendant and member of the Tangirnaq Native Village in Kodiak. She is the author of *In the Current Where Drowning Is Beautiful* (Wesleyan 2022) and *How to Dress a Fish* (Wesleyan 2019), shortlisted for the 2020 International Griffin Prize for Poetry and winner of the 2020 Colorado Book Award, and the linocut illustrated chapbook *Converging Lines of Light* (Flower Press 2021). Her poems have appeared in *Hayden's Ferry Review*, *Boston Review*, *Tin House*, *Gulf Coast*, *LitHub*, *Red Ink* and elsewhere. She currently teaches at the Institute of American Indian Arts and is an assistant professor at UMass Amherst.

from "DISQUIET ARK"
by Abigail Chabitnoy

ark, I'm afraid to tell you
how I've been waiting for you
to heave on these shores

like a promise no one should have required
from their god,
my chasms ravenous

and previously winged—

was it power or will
i was turned into a snake? that is
did i have any choice?

naturally i can smell my blood
when it comes

To reprint, reproduce or transmit electronically any portion of this book beyond brief quotations in reviews or for educational purposes, please make a written request to the publisher.

The 3rd Thing

editors@the3rdthing.press

Bookseller & academic distribution
is handled by Small Press Distribution, spdbooks.org.
Support the press and writer with your individual purchases
through the3rdthing.press.

Cover art by Barbara Earl Thomas,
detail of "In Case of Flood"

Cover & book design by
Anne de Marcken

Author photo, Jason Quigley

Abigail Chabitnoy retains the copyright to the excerpt of "DISQUIET ARK," which appears in this book as part of a Land Acknowledgment.

With thanks to Robin Wall Kimmerer and The University of Oregon Press for permission to reprint the excerpt of *Gathering Moss: A Natural and Cultural History of Mosses* that appears as an epigraph to this book.

Typeset in Cormorant Garamond and Century Gothic
Printed in the United States of America

ISBN: 978-1-7379258-3-5

LCCN: 2023938525

First Edition
2 4 6 8 10 9 7 5 3 1

SIFT

ALISSA HATTMAN

The 3rd Thing, Olympia, Washington

for my mother
Kathleen Jones Meyers

Much learning takes place by patient observation, discerning pattern and its meaning by experience. It is understood that there are many versions of truth, and that each reality may be true for each teller. It's important to understand the perspective of each source of knowledge. The scientific method I was taught in school is like asking a direct question, disrespect-fully demanding knowledge rather than waiting for it to be revealed. From Tetraphis, I began to understand how to learn differently, to let the mosses tell their story, rather than wring it from them.

Robin Wall Kimmerer

Gathering Moss: A Natural and Cultural History of Mosses

1

I thought that being inside would protect me, with its corners and its curtains, then a kindness took me by the throat and stretched me taut against the sky, beaming, and I found something more valuable than protection. If only you could have seen it, Mother. What light.

The Driver arrived with a crate and inside the crate were the last of the winter squashes—butternut, acorn, kabocha, sweet dumpling. It had been ages since I had eaten food from a vine, and I had so many questions, concerns. The Driver listened, then she said the best way to prepare kabocha was to cut out the insides and fill it with stars. I blushed and grew old with her, right there in the smoggy sunlight.

Long story short—I left with her, Mother. I went outside.

Here's another way to say it: I gathered up all that you gave me and bolted. Escaped into the toxic air with the only person I'd met who had learned how to keep living.

I remember blackened fields and a sky the color of cantaloupe. The air was full of smoke, but inside the vehicle—with its systems and its filters—we could breathe freely. I watched the flickering red skies turn into plumes of dark blue and the plumes of dark blue turn into rain and the rain turn into puddles and the puddles turn into ice and the ice turn back into puddles and the puddles into air. Certain cycles, flows. Observing is one way to go on.

The Driver and I shared the same road, the same vehicle, but we were both following the uneven edges inside our own minds. Hours dripped into the chasm between us.

Occasionally, I found courage enough to choke out a thought even though my throat was so thirsty. The Driver was kind. She taught me how to sift, to sip water from the air. *Stay very still*, she said. *Listen to everything thrumming. Inside too, you feel it?*

Sometimes I think about how far I am from my abandoned home, how this becoming has made me less animal and more vegetal, and when I think about this, I think of you, Mother, and wonder whether you would have lived this way too, had you known it was possible, and if you had known, whether we, as women, might have thrived like moss, parts and parcels. Now, as we've traveled through day and night and through dayless, nightless dark, I've grown hints of you up my back and have not always known if it is a comfort or a burden. Perhaps it is both.

It is no easy task. The trick is to keep the sips small. Teeny-tiny.

2

Remember when you said that the trauma of the old world was upon us? You were sitting on the kitchen floor, shoes kicked off, hair draped over your knees. You looked small, devastated. Remember how the days blurred—slow, slow and then quick? The fires, the raids. That moment when we thought we'd be safe. But then: heat, drought. Lockdown. Poisoned atmosphere. The new regime.

For years, we lived inside the house without you—the larder stocked with canned vegetables, old processed food. Cy taught me all the survival skills he could remember from Basic, but mostly we kept to ourselves. The shock of it all too hard to communicate. I'd sit for hours in what muted light broke through blackout curtains and try to understand. I'd call up memory like medicine—lying in the tall grass, the sun on my face before exposure was too dangerous.

The headaches were intense. My forehead felt as if it were splitting open, exposing me to something.

Many years passed. People died. You died. Then, one day, a knock at the door.

3

I write to you from the present, Mother. We sit together, you and I, here in this letter.

Why me? I ask The Driver about the crates.

You needed feeding, she says.

The Driver and I are passing through fields of ash. The day's drive has gone hot, ruddy and broke-open, spilling out.

I grew crop here, The Driver says, gesturing toward the burns. *Barley. Just last season.*

She says the word barley with such reverence. A loved one, now dead.

Where are we going? I ask.

To fertile soil, she says. *Soon there will be river. Then the land will get very dry before we reach trees, then mountain, then beyond mountain. That is my hope.*

And others?

Others? I can't say.

4

We drive and drive until we finally come to river. The Driver and I run barefoot down the revetment and plunge our faces into water. Here the air is clean, but the river is dirty. Even so, we drink until we are overfull. We sit on the edge of the concrete slope, thinking together now, trying to define this sudden expansion. The road, the river. We cannot touch the word for our condition. It is too vast.

The Driver becomes sick. She leans over and vomits water onto the pavement. The water is a small pond and in the pond are tadpoles and snails and black algae bottle caps slicked with half-memories and pain. I take up some of the water in my hands and watch The Driver's story swirl with my own.

Thank you, I say to the stories in the water that are not just our stories but also living creatures, the algae and the tadpoles, creatures with stories all their own.

Thank you, I say to The Driver, still ill. I am grateful that we are here together. I can see the acorn flush of her face peaking, sick with grief, and she sees me—sees my own story—sees the girl leaning against moss walls as spores grow up all around her.

Memory makes what it needs to make, The Artist once said at a talk. Remember when talks used to happen?

I remember looking at you in the mirror looking back at me looking at you. You were wearing cream-colored nylons. You prodded at your pinched skin and said that no matter what you try to suck in, something will always spill out. You showed me magazine images of women's bodies. This is the difference between real and airbrushed, you said. I couldn't focus—I imagined some man doing the impossible, painting the air—but, or maybe because of that, it was a lesson that stuck in me and grew.

Here's what I want to tell you about travel. First, you have to find the right partner. That person should be resolute and know when (and when not) to talk. They should embrace change, because just when you think you understand the vehicle, it changes, and just when you understand your partner, they will change, and the river will change, and our insides will change and it will make us sick and then maybe we will be well, if just for a moment, before becoming unwell again and that is the whole process in a nut. The secret to travel is pacing. Sip slowly. Another lesson I have learned is that you should choose a person and put your trust not in that person but in how you move and how you sit still together. It won't feel as it felt before, but no matter. This is not any indicator of rightness or wrongness. Watch. Can you see it? How the gaze sits, leaps?

I will also say that traveling is not as easy as it used to be. Sometimes The Driver and I are traveling in a truck, sometimes a helicopter, sometimes something else entirely. The vehicle changes as we change. It does not run on gasoline or diesel or electricity; it is something we call truck or helicopter for lack of a better word. The important thing is that we are together, moving.

Let it go, says The Driver.

I let the pond drain back down into the river but lovingly. The tadpoles grow into frogs as they swim away. What remains of the story? Glints, traces.

Once the sun has faded, and our lungs have fully absorbed the clean air, we lace up our leather boots, and head to the car.

The Driver gets into the passenger seat.

There is no other option—I drive.

POND SNAIL Homeish. Back heavy with spiral shell, the swell of life shimmering. Nearby, river. Nearby, beard of black algae. Belly slick over rock, slick slide over stone, the warm stone, earth vibrating. Slide belly stone, belly vibrating, a slim line. A slime line curved over stone. The spiral shape finds shelter at the center. Slide over and under and into what some might call sleep. Sadness is here, but is not all. Slide away, out of view, far from capture. The curvy wet line turns to shimmer.

5

I drive and drive, far away from the river, and past what used to be a city—charred buildings, burnt-out vehicles, piles and piles of sheet metal and broken brick. I'm all car as we speed through the remains.

Outside, the land grows flat and dry. I gradually return to myself.

The Driver slumps in the passenger seat. She releases a long moan that fills the car with a dark cloud of debris—ash, the dust of shell and bone, bottle caps again and always. The cloud is not the same as the pond. This grief seems old, ancient. I do not know why she suffers or how long it will consume her. I watch the dark air circulate, spiral and speckle the inside of the car. It is not so awful, to sit with her in this swirl, once I realize that her grief is a type of loving.

The project of breathing the dark air does not take long for me to learn, but it is hard to stay focused on the road. The drive stretches on and I am unsure when or if The Driver will go back to driving. I fear I may not be strong enough or wise enough to know how to keep going. All this smoke and debris make for terrible headaches.

When The Driver and I first fled, she was prepared. The truck was full of what we might need—sleeping bags, backpacks complete with pocket knives, gloves, first aid supplies. Not much water, but plenty of seed. Some crates of food: apples, rhubarb, squash, endive, and leeks. I was frightened, hesitant, but The Driver had the confidence of a comet. Now, our supplies have dwindled and our vehicle has shrunk.

The Driver has finally fallen asleep. My headache is awful, but I can still think, and so I think of you, of course. Often I think of how I failed you. Look around. There is nowhere to hide in the desert except maybe in a car full of smoke. Breathe, sip.

In moments of exposure, think of a river.

I draw up the river in my mind and that leads me to the river long ago, which leads me to the green grasses where you sat, cradling me, nursing. Birth was at once a miracle and pedestrian. A baby was born, an old woman crossed a parking lot with plastic bags of produce dangling from her wrists, acres of old growth were cut down for a highway, another baby was born. But, when I think, which is all I can do here in this vehicle, I think about how you made me from your body, and then your body made food, and you nursed me from your body, and I drank in one easy stream until I was full, and when I was full, you placed me naked in the grass, and the grass grew, and it was a home for the insects, and it was food for the snails, and when the grass was full it released air for every living thing that breathed, and I grew and grew, and you loved me as I changed, and when the world was falling apart and you struggled to breathe, I did not care for you as I should have because I did not know how, or I did not take the time to learn what caring for you meant, and what I mean to say now, in this silent smoke-filled car, with this grieving person next to me, sleeping, is that I am sorry for every casual or not-so-casual way I harmed you.

The sun sets and I drive within the muck of the cloud. The Driver and I breathe out and breathe in. The sun rises. The dark debris in the air settles into dust on the dashboard. My headache dulls into softer, greyer tones. The Driver blinks. Her whole being reminds me of a feather.

Look, she says.

A grey jagged line cuts into the sky and the sky cuts into the road and the road into us. My chest peels open and gasps.

Let's not be hasty, The Driver says.

We go quiet, pretending not to hope.

Still, I say the word loud and clear inside my head—*mountain.*

6

We come to the dunes. An impossible forever of alabaster sand rolling in ever-shifting mounds from here to nowhere. The wind writes stretch marks on the land. Sun, blinding.

The car has become a small aircraft—part balloon part buggy. It is easy to drive, but predicting the sand proves difficult. I learn how to razorback down windswept ledges, to search for the smoothest lines. Wind howls through the gaps in the glass cab. It throws me off track with its shrieking.

The Driver stares out at the dunes, refusing to take back the wheel. She snaps at me and then dozes. I don't know why she snaps, but the hunger and the heat cannot be helping. She has urged me to read patterns in the dunes, to be on the lookout for sinkholes. I squint, but I only see static. My mind races with possibilities that all end with the desert swallowing us up.

The dunes roll across the horizon in open waves. If it wasn't for the heat, you would think it was snow. *Just feel your way through*, I remember you saying. Your lesson for driving in a blizzard.

How is it possible, I ask The Driver. I do not understand her mood. She is all edges and corners.

How is what possible?

This brightness?

What brightness? What are you asking? Be direct.

Why is it white?

Why is what white?

The sand.

It is not white. It is clear, crystal.

It looks white.

The Driver sighs. Maybe she is tired of explaining. *You misinterpret the sand,* she says. *Your reading of it is too narrow, too self-involved.*

I am sorry, I say. I want to understand.

Well, she says, slow, so I get it. *Gypsum is clear. It only seems white because the many crystals are reflecting the sunlight.*

Gypsum?

From the mountains that rose up from the ocean.

I do not see the ocean.

The Driver stares at me. There is a fire in her, a center blaze.

Imagine a story that doesn't begin with you, she says.

I tighten my grip on the steering wheel and focus.

Imagine an ocean that existed, long ago. Imagine mountains growing up from the ocean floor and imagine that out of the many mineral compounds that make up a mountain that this one carried gypsum, and now imagine rain, so much rain, flooding down the mountain with nowhere to go, so it pooled, and when the earth grew hotter and hotter, and the lake dried up, it formed huge selenite crystals, and the wind blew for what felt like forever, and the selenite knocked around and broke into coarse compounds that became finer and finer—tiny crystals of sand.

Yes, I say, quiet. *I see it. And then we came with our oohs and ahhs and potato chip bags and tanks full of missiles.*

Yes, The Driver says, closing her eyes. *That is not so hard to imagine.*

The sand is beautiful, though, I say.

Don't try to make it better, says The Driver.

7

We have run out of water and our food supply is low. The mountains are farther away than we realized. The Driver tells me to stop at the next patch of cacti. It is hard to see anything through the pitted windshield. My headache has returned. A dull throbbing with dark floaters.

There! The Driver yells.

I slam on the brakes. The Driver jumps out and runs into the dunes.

My legs are wobbly and my throat is dry. It takes all my effort to trudge after her, to fight the wind. My head pounds, a constant thudding. Everything closes in.

You speak to me, Mother. There, in the thick of it. You say, *Love—go back.*

I say, *I cannot.*

You say, *Well—if you cannot—then you must not stop.*

The soft cradle of your voice is edged with thistles and thorns.

I pull myself together out of the dune, find my feet, huff up the hill. At the top, I scan the vast waves of sand, marbled in sky shadow. The Driver is nowhere, but I see a greenhouse. It is my desire for home and the person I would be if only I could get there. I go in.

The air inside is warm and gravid and clean. The rooms are lush with plant life that spirals from the ceilings, blooms from rocks, burrows deep into the ground. Globules of light slip down the surface of glass. My head is still pounding, lungs wheezing. I walk through the shimmer and follow a darkened hallway into a bedroom with ivy-covered mirrors. Shadows hover at the edges. So quiet I can hear the soil shift, leaves curl open and stretch, the lamellae of a gecko's feet scraping across the surface of a stone. I stare into a mirror at my reflection, at a cut on my forehead. The wound is filled with tiny star-shaped plants. This green organism that is many organisms, that is separate from me and also me, that is me and is new to me and is ancient. I reach out to touch the growing galaxy binding me together and get pricked.

I have no memory of this wound, how it happened.

Let me, says The Driver, who is now standing above me, waving her gloved hands.

I look back. The bedroom is gone and the greenhouse is gone. It is just me and The Driver and the sand and a cluster of barrel cacti that huddle together like a frightened family.

The Driver grips a cactus and twists it from the ground. A bunch of skinny roots dangle at the base.

You okay? she asks.

At first I think she is addressing the cactus. I nod, though my head is still foggy.

She places the cactus on a rock and takes her knife from her pocket. She chops off the bottom of the cactus and shows me the kiwi-colored inside. The middle ring shines.

Just have to get past the glochids, she says, turning the barbed creature around in her gloved hand. She stabs the knife through its side and skins the spines from the inside out.

It takes a while to notice taste, texture. Like watermelon, but without the sweetness. The Driver cuts into another. Cucumber with occasional grit. We drink this food until we are full.

The Driver stops. *What's that?* she says.

I cover my forehead with my right hand.

She cups her hand to mine. Tenderness. *Don't,* she says.

I let my hand fall into hers.

May I? she says.

I nod. My heart thrums.

Gently, she trails her thumb over my forehead. That part of me is oversensitive, soaks up too much of her.

Amazing, she says. *How could I have missed this?*

She looks into my eyes. *Mosses.*

This can't be good, I say.

It just is, she says.

Everything pulses. Staccato. I watch floaters dance in the sand spiral wind.

Don't worry, she says. *I'll drive.*

WESTERN BANDED GECKO Slips into the darkness between two stones and waits. Green eyes blink away light. Waits in trapped heat. Waits in layer of neck, layer of torso, layer of tail—loose. A gust of sand blows. Clay, bedrock, crust. Blink-blink. Teeth tear dead skin from body. Body swallows the dead skin self. Waits. A tiny tooth falls from mouth full of tiny teeth. An uncertain birth. Peels toes from the rock surface. Climbs back into light.

8

Remember how lovely it was to watch the woman at the grocery store? Her dark curls captured in a hairnet, her flour-powdered arms? How she chose our sourdough from the piled up loaves? *Sliced*, she said, knowing already what we liked.

Remember, at the end, how you said that breathing was a chore? *Like inhaling flour*, you said.

Bread aplenty. The slicer's hum, the blade. She slipped the sourdough into the plastic bag. One gold twist tie.

You said, *she smiles with her eyes*.

9

We drive deep into the night before pulling over to sleep. By morning the winds have dropped and the storm has cleared. We get out of the buggy to wipe the layer of sand off our windshield. In the distance—jagged mountain peaks.

Don't hope too hard, The Driver says. We get back into the buggy and drive.

I dream people. Whole communities growing crop together. Out the window, I watch the low murmur of plant life swell. Patches of bunch grass and scrub brush. The land is craggy as we near the mountain, but rich with vegetation. We stop to forage for food.

The Driver reads our surroundings as we walk. I watch wisps of cloud overhead. I have to remind myself to keep to her heels, stay grounded. She stops at a bush and examines some purple berries.

Not these, she says, and continues on.

We don't find much to eat. Some wild mustard greens. Pine nuts, onions. Eventually, we grow tired. We drink water from a spring and rest on a fallen log.

Something shimmers between two boulders.

The Driver digs down into the crevice, and pulls out a black garbage bag.

My chest blooms. *Do you think that—*

The Driver empties the contents on a flat boulder. We examine each relic—empty bottles of hand soap and sanitizer, some disintegrating ear plugs, a pair of toenail clippers, and a bunch of empty prescription pill bottles. Pepto Bismol. Hosiery. More plastic bags. A tube of toothpaste curled up into itself.

We should get back, she says.

I stuff the items into the bag and sling it over my shoulder, but The Driver thinks the bag should stay.

It's not ours, she says.

I return the garbage to where we found it, but keep the Pepto bottle.

The Driver wants to pretend our discovery is no big deal, but I can sense that she shares my excitement. On our walk to the vehicle, she cannot stop talking. She tells me stories about plants and small creatures performing the impossible. How flowers, sensing the vibrations of bees' wings, will increase the concentration of sugar in their nectar. *There are more ways to hear than with your ears*, she says. She tells me about a species of frog that can stay buried in mud, without food or water, for years. *Very adaptable*, she says, and then tells me she once saw a hermit crab scuttling across a boardwalk in a Tab can.

I do not know why she tells me these stories. It must say something about her own inner world, though I am not sure what. It is hard for me to focus. I would rather talk about the trash we found, the possibility of people.

But I don't press. I think about the crab in the Tab can. Us in our vehicle. I picture the bright pink can with the white modish label— crab claws clicking against the pavement.

10

Here, The Driver says. *Have some piñons.*

We chew silently. A sparrow lands on a sage bush.

When did you start farming? I ask.

After the first of the raids I settled for a while with some people who grew crop.

And your family?

The Driver looks at me. *Do these taste bitter to you?*

I pick through the nuts. *Sometimes I get one that's sweet.*

I was pretty young when my parents died in the Big One. My adoptive parents. I don't remember my birth parents. Don't know a thing about them. Don't want to. You'd have to be pretty messed up to bring a kid into this world.

She digs the toe of her boot in the sand, looks down. Her black hair is a curtain.

Must have been hard, I say.

I wait, but The Driver doesn't respond.

Is that it? I say, about the nuts.

We're in the desert, she says. *I can't work miracles.*

I pick up a small stone at my feet. It is grey with a fragment of a shell fossil. The stone is warm as a face.

Turn around, The Driver says. She unzips my pack and takes out one of the seed parcels. *Hold out your hand.* She doles out a dozen teardrop shaped seeds. *Pumpkin*, she says.

I look at the small pile. So light. So dead-seeming.

We need to save the rest for planting. She must think I want more.

I nod. *Hold out your hand*, I say. I place the stone in her palm. *It holds some of the ocean.*

She rolls the stone around in her palm, then puts it in her mouth and swallows.

That's not safe, I say.

She finds another stone and swallows that one, too. And then another.

She shrugs. *You do what you have to do.*

I feel granular, tiny particles of myself blowing away.

Do you feel that? I ask.

I feel so much right now, she says.

The separating, I say.

WILD MUSTARD The flowering weed is going to seed. Pod clusters, round and smooth, dark purple-brown. Hairs on the lower mid-vein of the pinnatifid leaves. Scent of clover. Of pepper. Ancestor of kale. Ancestor of cabbage. Ancestor of swiss chard. Of cauliflower, of turnip. A family before there was language for family. Everything related. Taproot thin, but hearty. In frost. In drought.

11

I have been thinking about that time we shared a pop in the kitchen nook. How you poured mine into a plastic cup, but it was too sweet for me to stomach.

The town hissed with dying mothers. Sky full of smoke. It was not the first time, nor would it be the last.

I was so small. I can still feel your hand on my shoulder. You closed the curtain. Cleared the table. When you returned, you had a glass of water, a paper bag, and a cheap watercolor set. I remember the rectangular plastic tray with its small egg-shaped wells of red, blue, green, yellow, orange, purple, and black. You handed me one plastic paintbrush and dipped the other into the water.

We'll make our own sky, you said.

Together we painted blue and yellow swirls on the bag. The colors were murky on the brown paper.

Who's the painting for? I asked.

Like a postcard you send to yourself.

What's a postcard?

It's how people know that you remember them.

Did you see how we were already starting to peel away from ourselves—who we were before—and from each other?

12

What do I mean to you?

The Driver doesn't answer. She's been distant, sunk deep inside herself.

Before I met you, I say, *I was stuck in my house, but even more I was stuck inside myself.*

We walk through burnt forest, charred ground covered in ash.

I'm not sure of who I am anymore, she says looking up into the purple sky.

I'm trying to tell you how much you mean to me, I say.

I hear you, sort of, but not fully. What you have said hasn't become part of me yet.

The moss on my forehead has dried up. Maybe died.

You are such a part of me, I say.

It's unforgivable, she says. About her birth parents, I think.

What do I mean to you?

The wind kicks up ash. I start to cough and cry and cough, so we both sit on a burnt stump until the fit passes.

13

The Driver is trying to work something out in her head. She worries over thoughts until they are a worn-down easy path.

That stuff in the bag could have been from ages ago, she says.

Maybe, I say, dipping the empty Pepto bottle into a ravine. I drink from the bottle and pass it to her. She seems surprised, then something else—maybe a little delighted that I rebelled against her wishes. *But sometimes people need to imagine life even when life is not there.*

It is dark by the time we return to the dune buggy. We are sweat-covered and filthy, but The Driver smells nice. Like sweet grass and wet clay. The moon throws shadows on her face, beautiful and weary. Together, we sleep.

We awake inside a parked helicopter, midday light trickling through the foggy windshield. The world is quiet except for the soft, hesitant song of a western bluebird.

The Driver is eager to get going. She tests out the stick and pedals, reads the panel.

I'm not sure about this, I say.

She starts up the motor and raises the collective. We hover as she manages the cyclic—forward and backward, left and right. We teeter in the air like a drunken dragonfly.

My heart races. As always, she walks me through it all in easy, measured breaths.

Every inch of me—spores budding and bursting. I take sips of air between thrill and panic.

The Driver lifts the collective and we rise.

From above, the burnt forest sprawls for miles and miles. The black trees look like porcupine quills on grey skin. Our helicopter shadow moves across the sharp dead things and bald patches.

14

This is what it's like to hover.

Like floating in water, bobbing up and down, but different. Jerkier, odd. To hold a position, but not to touch. To be suspended, but also moving. To be of the air. To loom, to imply. A hummingbird. A ghost.

It will feel like you are stuck, but you are not stuck. You are beholding.

15

Remember that day you took me to the field? You slathered me in SPF50. I wore your favorite band shirt, too big for me but I still felt cool. There were pockets of people under umbrellas and canopies or huddled in the shade of one big oak. Bikinis, shorts. The smoke was in the distance that day. The sounds of laughter trickled through the air, air humming with bass. A band not far off.

You set up the open tent and instructed me to eat ice cubes if I got too hot.

If you were to ask me now, what I miss most is the possibility people hold, how each person contains new stories, new attitudes, a new education. How much I could learn and feel and evolve (or devolve, depending) with each conversation. I miss both the up-close and the far-off potential, the bright-color blur of groups of people congregating, expressions I'd like to see closer, and then again, and then to understand.

You returned with new friends carrying homemade ginger beer and artesian well water in mason jars. One woman had peachy cheeks and a husky voice, her right arm covered in bandages. Another man smelled like jerky and talked to me as if I was part of the crowd. He said, *What do you think of this song? Too mellow?*

Cy had been drafted. The danger was still in the air—something we could not quite place, a type of normalized trauma that had taken over our lives. That day felt out of time, though, from days before.

Stolen. You seemed calm, joyful.

It was quiet at first, the song. Harmonies, bitter and pure. Then, drums. Guitar. Cymbals. Screaming.

The peachy woman said, *The stars sleep under us tonight.*

16

If I were a watercolor postcard, I'd be promising but lacking in focus. Amateur. I would arrive in your mailbox weather-worn. Blurs of greens smeared into brown—I might be a pinecone, or the life cycle of a frog, or a portrait of grief, or someone's lost scarf prominently placed on a fence by a kind stranger. I'd be full of wispy, emotive *f*s and *t*s. A bunch of broken open *o*s. Illegible. I would be the type of postcard that is all feeling—the kind of extra-sense that people call nonsense—and all the feeling would spill into you in a manner only you could interpret. Our private language. A blur.

I miss you, Mother.

17

The roaring whir of the helicopter pulsates through my body. We dip and dive. The Driver manages skillfully.

I imagine, if I opened The Driver's head and walked around in there, I would see her knowledge arranged into a billion carefully woven baskets, all containing terminology and words I cannot pronounce, and that the willow or wisteria or animal hair that made up the baskets would connect to other baskets in a dense bramble that only she could decipher. Still, I am starting to see it—her intricate mind, her great design.

Have you ever woven a basket? I ask, yelling over the sound of the blades and the engine.

No, she says. *Why?*

I just imagined your mind as a billion baskets of knowledge, I say.

She mulls this over. *I like that*, she says.

We teeter to the right as The Driver attempts to stabilize. Something rises up from the oldest part of my gut. I go woozy, lightheaded. The floor vibrates. I try to concentrate on my boots—skin inside skin.

Here's how to find your body—

Don't hold your breath or inhale suddenly. Sip water. Use earplugs.

Chew on ginger or mint, if you have it. Tilt your head into turns. Look to the horizon.

The Driver smiles at the controls. She seems to be enjoying this new education.

It doesn't seem like you're angry anymore, I say.

She looks at me and says, *What do you mean?*

At your birth parents, I say, and immediately I wish I could capture the words and stuff them back down.

She looks at the windshield, stung.

We travel through a cloud. Bile rises from my stomach.

The Driver starts to cough. Coughs and coughs into her left hand.

Here, she says.

She hands me three stones. I roll them over in my palm.

Other tips: Find a pressure point on your inner wrist. Invent verbal placebos, such as This Will Not Kill Me. Focus on a grounding object. Like a stone.

CLOUD DEBRIS Light against light and light in air. Light on light voice. A fragile air made of ash. Bottlecap memory burn. Light and floating. Dead voice. Light on light voice. Crushed bone voice. Voice that is light and light that is ever shifting—how to survive. How to survive ash. How to survive smoke. How to survive light ever shifting. How to live inside bone dust.

18

The Artist's talk was a beautiful arrangement. Orchestra of information. It was about corners, Book 20 in the *Odyssey*, memory, The Artist's father's dementia, Cassandra, Bachelard, and unboundedness. I took many notes because I wanted to remember what she was saying and I knew the act of writing would help it stay in my head.

Memory makes what it needs to make.

I had to travel a long distance by foot to get to the attic room and had a story about searching for my missing brother if anyone were to stop me and ask why a young woman was out past curfew. I kept quiet. Strangers watched me walk by, but no one asked questions.

The directions took me to a house behind another house. There, I was led up some stairs, through a hidden door, into a small room with about twenty folding chairs and a podium. I sat in the back and quietly waited. Some light filtered in through the curtain of one small window. Cobwebs in the rafters.

Eventually, The Artist took her place behind the podium. She wore a light blue blouse and a light brown blazer. Her glasses rested on her nose. Red frames. During her talk, she would occasionally glance up at us, her small audience—none of whom I knew—to see if we were understanding, or to provide a look or a pause in a manner that felt very much like a good friend revealing something scary or hard.

When the unboundedness comes after you, when you can't escape outwardly because it is already inside, and already burning, then you really have no shelter.

Now where can I go?

There were three brown buttons up each sleeve of The Artist's blazer. Her voice was achy, reaching. When she shifted, the floorboards underneath her creaked. She held the papers she read from, and as she came to the end of the page and turned it over face down on the podium, I could see there were photographs of women. Who were they?

Unboundedness is a rope not tied off at the end to prevent its unraveling.

That night The Artist talked about how corners can be shelter, but they can also make you feel trapped. Then she mentioned something about the need to be cornerless, but I was not sure I understood. The last part of The Artist's lecture was about experiencing The Ganzfeld Effect.

I remember thinking that I would need to go to Germany to understand what she meant, but of course I never had the chance.

It floods with its simplicity — the white light deprives you of navigating clues — a strange pressureless pressure — their livingness was going at a different pace than mine —

I understand what she described—the disorienting effect—the simplicity, the pressure, the pace—it is what life feels like now.

19

The sky is cornerless. We are unbounded. The mountain is a dark idea of shelter in the middle distance.

I watch The Driver manage like she always manages. Her jaw, her focus, her wonder. I, however, am dizzy with memory. Thoughts float by—a slow, looming quality, cumulonimbus. Perhaps this is the nature of flying. I am thinking of all those I have not heard from for so long, or those who died without being heard. I allow words to filter through my mind.

On gossamer wings, the darkness drifting in—

Nana May reclining in her olive green chair, stocking feet resting on the ottoman. *O weary traveler rest—The blue above; the blue below— Settle gently on the waves.* She eats grapes from a small pink bowl. *Floating over the stillness—Beneath her heart the little bud—Lies waiting, to be unfolded.* Every word like prophecy. *Leaf struggling against a whirl- pool—Thistle floating down a deep abyss—To rest upon the moss so cool.*

To rest. *Pitted against the sky.*

Do you remember, Mother? Her inscription in the book with the blue cover: *Bless you, Our Baby—you will make us all—so happy—Bless you again, Nana May.* You didn't share her certainty, to expect this of a child. Bless you for not asking this of me.

Our baby, our baby.

Remember Ira born into the world without the ability to swallow or breathe? *A terrible love*—what the mother of the mother said at the funeral. All the marigolds had fried in the sun that year, so for the memorial you draped our home with lavender ribbons and cream-colored curtains. Baked bread with sesame seeds and set out pitchers of clean water and enough glasses for everyone. We sat in chairs or leaned on the balcony that overlooked the red cedar and the small mound of fresh dirt, marked with flat heart-shaped stones. By then you didn't give a whit that funerals had been outlawed. We gathered, we placed our stones, we laid down our grief. It was summertime. The air was good.

At the time, when you were still trying to learn what to do, how to organize, we listened to speeches from long-ago activists. The Labor Leader, I remember, spoke in soft, measured tones over the radio. *The working conditions are brutal . . . no toilets . . . no drinking water . . . too many speed-ups . . . four tons of grapes in one day.* I thought of Nana May eating those store-bought grapes. Did she know? I wanted to know. What does four tons of grapes even look like? *The brutalization of the human body . . . you have to protect them from the insecticides or their skin will fall off . . . if you try to defend your rights or the rights of your children you get fired.*

These things are kept very quiet . . .

Beneath her heart the little bud—

Together, we figured out the math. Four tons equals 240 cases of grapes, equals roughly 2,880 bottles of wine. One person, one full day of their life, $8. *You have a direct line to the growers, a direct line.*

What remains? A long-frayed rope. Rest, little bud.

PEPTO Any neglect, any pink residue, any scrap or rot or rubble or waste, supposing the echo of flux, melt, minty scent fading, suppose the swill evaporates, suppose dilapidation, bulbous, suppose the edges soften into dirt patterns, suppose the song of chalk written in rivers, suppose a plastic meadow, semi-permanent neglect, suppose a breakdown, a lost libretto for debris.

20

Nana May's message to her kin—*you will make us happy*—felt less like a hope and more like a command. The baby she wrote to was surely a girl.

The sun is starting to set as we pass over rocky terrain.

We are not far now, yells The Driver.

I feel nauseous, but take comfort in watching her grip the cyclic. She has long, elegant fingers, perfect for a pianist (if only she had been born into another world). Nails bitten to the quick. The helicopter—the up and down of it all—gives me the spins. When I lean in, all I can see is childhood.

Do you remember, Mother? The puddles in the shag carpet of our basement? The puddles, the men.

The men arrived and they stayed. When I told the people our story, they said *that did not happen*. When I went to others, I was ignored. *Prove it*, they said. I brought in the photos of your ribs, your back. I wrote out all the details. I told the story again—the men, the men, the basement puddles. The people said, *We are sorry about your story, but so much time has passed. What can we do about it now?*

I roll the stones over in my hand. The nausea passes.

21

The photo was taken during The Great Depression. That is all I know. I found it in a book I once loved, *The Piazza Tales*. Though I no longer have the book or the photo, I will do my best to describe it from memory—

There are three white boys roped to a tree. The youngest has no shoes. He is wearing a diaper. The other two look to be the same age, maybe six or seven. One has blond hair and a cowlick. He is looking over his shoulder at the field. The other has dark hair. Though his arms are bound, his fingertips reach up toward the rope in a broken awkward way, but I know they are not broken. He is just reaching. The youngest is the only one who looks into the camera. There is either terror or hunger in his eyes, I'm not sure. Maybe both. The leaves of the tree have all fallen. There is a hazy light at the top corner of the photo, perhaps a smudge on the lens.

Whatever those boys did, they were punished. Back then a photo marked the event as if it were a holiday. Christmas or the Fourth of July. The photo seemed to say, *Finally, that old tree could be put to good use.*

These boys were not the men who took you away. The men—for the life of me, I cannot remember their faces. Instead, I think of this photo.

The puddles the men, the men the boys, the boys the tree. Oak, if I remember right.

22

The stones are heavier now and slippery. I struggle to hold them. I am reminded of how obedient I can be.

Green shag carpet. The men reached up from the depths and pulled me under.

Once upon a time I was very good at crawling up into myself and watching it all from the secret attic of my mind.

I had to find new ways to survive.

Look—there is nowhere to hide in the air except maybe behind an expression, a cloud. The Driver has fallen out of focus. She cannot navigate both me and the wind. She ignores my cries, sudden and burbling.

I draw up a river in my mind. Death was at once a miracle and pedestrian. A baby died, a person in all white sliced what used to be a pig into paper-thin folds, a metal tower drilled down and then up from the earth, bottlecaps on the eyes of the dead. But, when I think and think, which is all I can do here in this vehicle, I think about how the men made me by pulling me under, and while I was under, by feeding me lies that I absorbed in one easy stream until I'd forgotten what was, and when I'd forgotten what was, they placed me on the wet carpet, violently on the carpet, the half of me that remained, and when I was trying to stitch the knowing back together, you did not care for me like you should have because the knowing was in pieces, or because you did not understand how to care, or could not care, not in your state, and what I mean to say now, here, holding these stones, with The Driver beside me, navigating, is that it hurt—it all hurt, but how you hurt me was the worst hurt of all.

There, I said it.

Of course, they hurt you too. So you hurt me by doing nothing and later I hurt you by doing nothing and on and on and on and—

River. Puddles.

I want out of this contraption.

I look over at The Driver. Her face is a blurry mess of colors inside shadows. I see she is screaming at me, but there is no sound.

I know, in that moment, we are going to die.

23

Then, a horrible accident—we survive.

24

A dripping sound. Light flickering against a wall of rock. We are inside a chamber of mountain. The helicopter has turned into a glass lantern with a warm, persistent glow.

The Driver lies motionless. I lean into her neck. Her sweet grass scent has faded. I hold her hand and murmur the breathing lessons she taught me. Each word a half-hum, a hope.

Listen to the thrumming, do you hear it?

Drip drop drip.

The Driver wheezes. I think she is dying. Her skin feels scaly, tight.

I slip my hand into her pocket and pull out the knife. Before panic sets in, before I can understand the impulse or the risk, I cut small slits into The Driver's chest, just below her neck, into the translucent layer of skin that is stretched so taut. She does not bleed. Beneath, there is another layer of skin. The new skin is shiny and looks soft. Her wheezing quiets.

I understand that all I can do now is wait.

In her ear, I whisper the lullaby you used to sing to me. A watery song about a silver moon and a boat and dreams.

Sail, baby, sail, out across the sea—

Parts of me break away, but I am not afraid. I am sure that, wherever she is, she feels it too, this fracturing.

only don't forget to sail, back again to me.

25

A memory. I'm sixteen. I sit in a field of dead grass. I can hear the men laughing, splashing in the river, our river, not far from the house. You are there with them, laughing. It is another day of fire warnings. Trees blaze not far off. The air is ashen.

In the field, I am alone. Safe. From here I can track the sound of the men and know they are far away from my body. They laugh. You laugh. Here, I can think. I do not need to be any one way for you or for them. No one knows where I am.

I hear you laughing, laughing, then I hear you scream.

I tried, Mother, but I froze. Too afraid to move.

Time passed. I told myself a story that a child would tell in order to explain a thing that cannot be explained. You were tired of me. You chose to leave.

Two years later they returned you to your bed, when you were too weak and damaged to be any use to them. Why did they bother? Was there feeling between you? Again, I documented what I could before giving up.

You spent days and days in your bed, recovering. You were only half there. I was angry. Your absent eyes felt like another abandonment.

So, I left you there.

26

Three regrets:

Not fighting for you/us.

Leaving you to recover alone.

Later, not caring for you while you were dying.

27

I am in the mountain. Somehow I am still holding the stones. I can hear the earthworms digging passages below my body. It feels comforting and lonely. Beetles turn over dirt. My mind turns over the crash. Perhaps this was no accident. Maybe this is what The Driver wanted. She's grown tired of me, our life together. Maybe I shared of myself too deeply. My brain chews and chews. The silent scream. The bright quality of light, too painful to look at directly. My head throbs.

My heart turns over. How do we face the unremembered truth? How can we possibly heal, go on?

The Driver, who I can tell is no longer just the driver, has stopped wheezing. Her body breathes easily. Skin upon skin. Copper-colored tissue paper, layered, translucent. I wonder who she is now.

BARREL CACTUS Midday windstorm. A spiky ribbed plant with a crown of fine spines. Gust of wind. Sand skitters across sand. Beetles scrape softly. Light warms every surface, then the winds die down. The bugs stop digging. A ripple in the air. Silent, hot. Very few survive.

28

The men come. Large puddles form in the basement. Shallow, then deep. Do you see them, Mother? The men leave. Take you. The puddles remain. There is no avoiding their murkiness. I try to walk around the puddles, but they seep up my legs and body and throat and under my eyelids and into my lungs. The puddles are slicked with a stain.

29

When I wake, the woman who is no longer just The Driver is gone. This does not alarm me. She has taken the lantern. The darkness is complete. I listen to water drip and the earthworms at work. I am learning to love this world.

The woman returns. She is many people.

You must remember to eat, they say, pulling the seed pouch from their pack.

I try to focus on their eyes and go dizzy.

This might be hard for me to get used to, I say.

This?

There are so many of you.

Eat, they say.

They hand me some of the seeds. Small and dry. They smile a series of smiles. Lamellae. I realize this is their name. They are many. Many ages, many genders. Ghosts. Ideas.

Are we dead? I ask.

Lamellae looks down at their arms.

Let's go, they say.

30

We walk through the dark, taking turns holding the lantern.

L tells me about the eons of dripping water that created the formations that look like gigantic teeth biting up from the rock floor.

We keep hearing the dripping sound. Together we say *drip* for each drop we hear. Our voices join the drops. Drip *drip* drip *drip* drop. Like this, time passes.

Something is happening, I say to L, showing them my forehead.

They have been busy, L says. *They're following genetic instructions for repair. It's remarkable. Not many organisms have the ability to revive from an air-dried state.*

We are of new minds these days. Our conversations slowly unfurl. We ask more questions of each other and it is, at once, both exhausting and exhilarating.

When did you first see purple? L asks me.

I close my eyes and think. I am unsure about the first time, the absolute first time, but I tell them a story about an action figure my brother had when he was still young, still alive. A villain, in purple and blue.

Why were purple and blue evil colors? I ask L. They do not answer. Instead, they ask: *What did the figure look like?* They are in a question-asking mood.

He had a skull for a face, but he had the body of a blue muscular man. He had a purple sword, purple battle staff with a ram's skull, and purple chest armor with crossbones. He always looked like he was squatting. Maybe because of all his muscles, I'm not sure.

Why do you think you remember this? they ask.

I am quiet, contemplative. The air is cool. We are traveling still, though it does not feel like it. We move so slowly. Drip drip drip.

I think it was because I was scared of the skull. The purple and blue reminded me of rot and the skull reminded me of death. I was especially scared of death when I was young but, then again, it was a different time.

Lamellae looks at me meaningfully. They are thinking, or maybe imagining. I am not sure.

I haven't always felt this way about purple, I say. *Once I saw a jacaranda tree in full bloom and it was not rotting, or evil. I saw it and I was overjoyed.*

The plastic man and the blossoms, L says. *What do you think it means?*

I do not know, I say. The dripping slows. *I suppose it has something to do with time passing.*

Have you ever tried to step inside purple?

I have! I say, delighted by this question. *By way of a shimmery evening dress.*

L smirks their many smirks. Their coppery layers are thrilling.

31

Mother, meet Lamellae. To me, they are miraculous. They are very good at narrowing their focus to stay alive. They are many kinds of beauty. The Driver, with her acorn skin, warm and bright, is often who I see most clearly, but there are many, many others from L's past, who comfort, who cling.

As I describe them, I lose them. They hide from me, from us, and I try not to blame them for hiding.

32

I feel the *us* of us drawing closer. We are learning our new bodies together. I dream we have a kind of sex.

L guides my hand down their torso—prickly then soft then slick. They bite at my jaw as I slip deeper into their wetness. Vision blurs. There is a hot pulsing in my head, euphoric, terrifying, much too much, but before I become completely absorbed, L leads my other hand over all their cuts, the procedure. At first I do not understand, but then they moan, both my hands working as they moan, and it is like a new kind of breathing, how they sigh and whimper, their glossy skin opening and closing and opening.

Rain trickles into paths between stones. L finds my lips and kisses deeply, runs their wet fingers over the stars of my forehead—quick, but gentle. My body shudders, a type of gasp, expansive.

I wake in lantern glow, in the trickle. Above us, I hear rustling. Bats adjusting their feet, readying their wings. Chiroptera. A word that L has taught me. I feel them communicate with each other. Dizzying, electric.

Echolocation, L says. *Not for us.*

I so desperately want an orienting language. Connection.

COSMOS Be planted, tethered, rooted. Be still. Still and straight, face toward the sun. Let the warm rays soak at the edges. Be leaves, uncurling, open, light. Be petal. Then wind. Then a chill moonglow. Be shifting from below. Roots stretching, with other roots, insects burrowing. Be raindrops. Dirt expanding, breathing. Be roots drinking in the sunshine for joy-stretch, then be as the earth contracts, tight at the roots. Warm, then too warm, then parched. Be thirsty, then cool. Be rustling, petals. Vibrations, then, in the air. Tiny buzzing. Be the sweetness that sound produces. The scent of nectar, strong, powdery, earthy, and blooming. Be inside the buzz. Here now. There there. The earth shifts.

33

Tiny waterfalls slip down the rock walls and into the earth. Trickle sounds throughout, chattering. I hear people murmuring.

I say this to L one evening, as we sip water and algae through the cracks of the mountain. The earth tastes sweet.

There was something I wanted to ask you, L says. *But I can't remember what it was. Something about stories.*

A story from childhood? I say.

No, not childhood, L says. *Something wet, something recent.*

Everything here is wet, I say.

Do you see the waterfall writing? L says.

I look at how the trickles of water cut paths into the stone. *Yes,* I say.

Ah, I remember! The pond, they say, so brightly that for a moment it feels like I have The Driver back.

The one you coughed up?

Yes, tell me, L says. *What happened exactly?*

POND Dead things float on the surface, but underneath the weeds sway. Tiny minnows swim through feathery green fronds. Sands shift. Fish the color of ink sip-kiss the sediment. A swirling shell slinks over grey and purpled stones. Minnows, all glass and entrails. The green creature dives head-first into ground, then shoots up, and skids across the top like it might be eating bits of debris. Floats there, bobs. Riverweed sways. The skin of the water reflects another world.

34

You and I sit in that coffeeshop near the old church park where people had made homes inside their tents. By then you had taken me out of school and we spent our mornings making lists, contacting allies, reviewing maps, assembling go bags. Sometimes we would bake muffins that we'd hand out to people on our way to the shop where your friend worked. I think I knew you didn't really have much of an escape plan, but I felt love and connection in the routine that you'd made for us.

We are sitting on stools at the bar. It is winter, just after the election. The air quality in the café is Orange, Unsafe for Sensitive Groups. You read to me from a magazine, an article where The Writer wrote about a conversation she had with her artist friend—

I was depressed, The Writer had said to her friend. *I could not even write.*

No! The Writer's friend had said to her. *This is precisely the time that artists go to work.*

I took note. I documented what we read, the weather, the feeling in the air. I thought that maybe, someday, I would arrange it all in a way that would help me understand what had happened.

You read aloud. The Writer wrote about how she had felt foolish in front of her friend—

I recalled the artists that have done their work in gulags, prison cells, hospital beds; who did their work while hounded, exiled, reviled, pilloried.

...in times of dread, artists must never choose to remain silent.

I made you read it again. I wrote down the words and repeated them in my mind with the hope that they would become part of my body—

I know the world is bruised and bleeding, and though it is important not to ignore its pain, it is also critical to refuse to succumb to its malevolence. Like failure, chaos contains information that can lead to knowledge—even wisdom.

We were going to be like those women—The Labor Leader, The Writer. We came so close.

35

The scratchy shifting in the center of my head is me, but not me. It is the mosses, alive, drinking. When the moisture and airflow are right, I feel like there are some things I understand. I wonder if they overhear my awkward translation. Something about our rhythms matches. Our movements slow. We are clumsy, but in the way that community—any community—is clumsy, and there is value in the clumsiness, this half-understanding. Maybe the attempt alone sustains us.

36

L names the orogenic cycle of the mountain. It has to do with defor-
mation and metamorphism and magmatism. They use other words
like *batholiths* and *suture zones*. All I hear is deep sadness.

Tell me a story, I say.

I am telling you a story, L says.

Tell me about something closer. What are you feeling?

L stops.

You want me to tell you about my parents, they say.

I care for you, I say.

L says nothing. They start walking without me. After a long silence,
they stop again.

Do you remember what happened? L asks. Their voice is a light breathy
timbre.

I can see The Driver, under all the layers, afraid.

The crash? I say. I shake my head. *I don't know. You were screaming.
But I couldn't hear it.*

Screaming? The Driver's mouth quivers, or flickers.

Then we were inside the mountain. Whatever it was—it feels huge, you know? Devastating.

I don't know, The Driver says, sinking behind L's many faces.

My body is a worn-down, brittle thing.

I wish you hadn't left me, Mother. I wish I hadn't left you.

37

You woke me in the middle of the night to show me the list.

Items for a Go Bag:

Water: 3-day supply

Food: 3-day supply

Warmth: emergency blanket, warmers, small tent

The Body: first aid/medical kit, pain relievers, medical gloves, prescriptions

Air: N95s and gas masks

Light: flashlight with batteries, matches

Information: AM/FM emergency radio with batteries

Support: whistle, work gloves, boots, clothes, pocket knife

Proof: medical information and IDs

Connection: list of emergency contacts, including an out-of-country contact

Memory: photos, notebooks, pencils, postcards, baby blanket, Snuggles

I got these bags, you said, showing me the sturdy backpacks. *We'll start packing tomorrow.*

I slept. When I woke the next morning, you were still there in my bed, holding me, holding the list.

38

As we get deeper into the mountain, L stops naming the faults.

I fill the silence with stories. Spiral into rumination.

L cuts me off, mid-memory.

I once had a friend, they say. Jonas, who had to have his leg amputated. He told me that there were always hard days, but none as hard as the days he spent longing for his leg, wishing for what used to be. It would not let him grieve, the wish. Or, to say it another way, it would not let him live. But, after many years, he started to accept that his leg was gone. He let the absence in, and the suffering that was once caused by the longing cleared a space for the grief.

I let L's story of Jonas sift through my body. Breath. I think of L's grief. The river, the cloud, the ocean.

I pull the stones from my pocket and put them back in L's palm.

WOOD FROG   Weather cools and body says *dig*.
Squeezes front digits to make a spear, trowels through
surface, nosing into warm blue bed of dirt. Body says
dig. Quiet down below. No hunger. Very little air. Body
listens. Insects tunnel through silty mud, earth shifts,
roots stretch. Heart slows, body slows. Deep fatigue.
Time blinks in and out. Freeze. Crystals form on outer
layer of organs. Cells change. Slumber. Dreams of water.

39

We change a little or a lot and I'm starting to understand that you cannot know a person so well.

We have stopped eating. All that we have left are a couple stalks of rhubarb, some of the berries we found in the desert, and the pouch of seeds, dwindling. We haven't rationed enough. We have grown thin. We have stopped menstruating.

L and I barely talk. When L does speak, their words are sharp and cold. We bicker in horrible loops. How maybe we should have gone this way or that, maybe we should turn around. We yell and cry at each other for what feels like days until we finally collapse into angry slumber.

The way has narrowed. The lantern is now a small pickaxe. We slip through waterways, widen fissures in stone.

We can't see one another.

Maybe we need the darkness, I say.

L doesn't respond. I can feel a fury growing inside them.

40

I've been having nightmares of L killing me in my sleep. In one dream, I am walking through the darkness and feel something soft and wet slip across my back, like a fallen cobweb. I mention it to L, but they don't respond. I cannot feel their body next to mine and I wonder if they've finally left me. I walk and walk, lonely and sobbing, a terrible center ache. Then I see a cloud of moving lights, like fireflies circling. I walk and walk but the cloud seems farther and farther away. I am convinced that the cloud is L. I want so desperately to see them. Then I sense something from above and a rock comes down on my head. I can feel the blood pooling, life draining from my body.

In the dream, I scream your scream, Mother. The river scream. An animal cry. But it is also L's scream. Silent. The pain is excruciating, until it's not. As I'm dying, I realize it is L who killed me, there in the dark. I am sure of it.

41

I have developed a practice. During our times of rest, I try to just be. Sometimes this means being inside my fear of L. I pull the feeling around my shoulders like a blanket, and sit there for as long as I can, and I watch the crimson color spread down my arms and my legs, seeping into my veins and arteries, terrified that it will consume me. Only it doesn't. The fear dissipates and I am left cold and alone in my sadness. Sometimes, then, I can finally fall asleep, but if I cannot fall asleep, I will lie awake and listen to L breathe and imagine how the ground below them might feel similar to the ground below me.

Sometimes I think about our house, Mother. I open the door and then I open another door and then I go down the stairs and around a corner and into the shocked silence that left me vacant, cold. And then I remember that we have never been safe.

I would not trade this for the house.

FIREFLY A light inside skin. Light for light's sake. Seed light. Breeze light. Light lost. Light without fire. Conscious light. Patient light. Light settling, slowing, silencing. Light dimming. Always, the skin. Stillness. Light dimming. Night dipping. Skin shifting. A scratch, an opening into the beautiful darkness.

42

Mother, this is the story of when I heard a knock at my door. Of what happened to me in that moment. It is too complicated for me say now, but it changed me. It was an old sound. My body remembered it. An entire story in that knock. Perhaps someday when my mind is clear I will be able to draw for you a map, simple, easy to follow even in the dark. You will hear the sound. A knock on your door. You will come out. Back to me. And what I mean by you, is the feeling of connection that I remember.

43

I wake and L's hands are glowing. I can see their faces and all of the fear melts away.

Their hands are cupped together around something—light bursts from between their fingertips.

Bioluminescence, they say.

Where did you find it? I ask.

It was just there next to me, flitting about. L looks at me, soft, their faces dancing in the light. *It is a wonder.*

Have I ever told you about Ira? I ask.

They shake their head.

Mother had these friends, a man and a woman. A couple. They came to our home for every special occasion. One year they arrived with a full dish of food and announced their engagement. They had a lovely wedding. Both of their fathers were still alive, both gave toasts. This was after the first of the big fires, but before the invasion. Then, the next year, they brought food again and announced that they were going to have a baby. Their sweet faces radiant, in love. But there were complications. Ira was born in July with an autoimmune disease. July—it sounds strange to say it out loud. Were there once months? Years? For weeks the couple fought to keep the baby alive, but he suffered. Every day, Mother visited, and every day she came home crying about how the doctors would not help. One night, after returning from who knows where, she shoved a package into my hands. I can't do it, she said. I knew that I was meant to deliver the package to Ira's parents and I knew whatever was inside the package would put an end to Ira's pain. She said, Be sure they read the directions. It's all there. I darted through dark neighborhoods, afraid, unsure of who I was becoming, who Mother was now. When I arrived, I could hear the baby's sharp, shallow cries. I found the father holding him. Weeping. The mother beside them. The baby struggling to breathe.

It happened. I delivered the package. I reminded them to read the instructions. I left. It happened—I had to keep saying it to myself—my brain constantly resisting. Horrible. Surreal.

We are silent.

It's remarkable, I finally say.

What? L says. *The couple, their courage?*

Yes, and—

L stops, sucks in some air. I do the same. It is hard and frigid, this air.

I know that the story is not Ira. But the story keeps him alive. He is present. Here is Ira. He is with us. And all the others are with us, you know? Here and now, in this moment.

L drops their hands open. The light goes flying off into darkness.

44

We have to fight, The Activist said. Remember that summer I volunteered at a youth summit on climate justice. Cy had been at war for a year by then so I must have been 13. I watched from backstage as she spoke.

We have to fight. That is, of course, why you are here.

I thought about Cy fighting for what some people called resources. The Activist wore a copper brown shirt and a vest, long hair loosely tied back. She told us to have courage to let go of what they have put in our heads and urged us to develop a worldview that spans thousands of years. It's what Lamellae was saying in the desert when they were still just The Driver. The Activist talked about how we live in a society based on empire, conquest, and how it is not sustainable. She reminded us that we are all interconnected.

Our relatives have fins and roots. Paws. Hooves. Wings.

The air quality in the building was at Yellow. I took bites of a strawberry oat bar as she talked. I had been assisting the deck lighting technician all day and I was hungry.

We make paupers of our relatives. We drive them to extinction and call it "Darwin." Her arms mimed the explosion to signify the enormity of this violence, like a bomb. *No. It's public policy.*

Someone from the audience shouted *Yes!* The crowd burst into applause, whooping and whistling. Even from backstage, I could tell they were energized. So was I. Ready to fight.

We are here, she said, as she waved an arm through the air.

Then, her mic was cut. I could see the audio engineer flailing in the control room before the auditorium went dark.

It wouldn't be long before the lights were back. Two, maybe three minutes. We'd see the podium, empty. A nervous person in a suit would stand in front of us and say that The Activist was needed elsewhere.

But, in that moment before the lights came back, no one *did* anything. Minutes before we had been ready to fight. And then we just sat in the darkness, afraid.

This darkness is so much more complete. Only each other and ourselves to fight.

45

I am starting to hear sounds that I did not hear when we first entered the mountain. I'm not sure if it is because these sounds weren't there or because my other senses are heightened because I've lost use of my eyesight. I lean into the qualities and textures of darkness. It feels silken, shiny if shiny were a feeling. I trust it.

L breathes in sharp breaths as we walk, determined as always. I desperately want something inside them to open. As if something inside me depends on it. I imagine L speaking of their resentment toward their birth parents, their grief for their adoptive parents, their anger at existing, and I imagine listening and telling them about my own wounds. I imagine we go back and forth like friends. I imagine this helps. If we are not friends, then what kind of companions are we? Maybe they do not trust me. Maybe I do not trust them. Surely I trust them. Why did they choose me?

These are the kinds of circles you draw in your mind when you've been walking forever through a mountain. I follow the hurt into the dark as if it is a light.

I can hear L's feet, but part of me senses that they are not there.

I let them do things to me, I say. *I let the men do what they wanted.* I bounce my words off of the place I think L might be. Wait for a reaction. *It seemed, at the time, that it would be less scary than to fight.*

L stops, so I stop.

Why are you telling me this, they ask.

Because, I say. *We are connected.*

You expect too much from me, they say.

We need each other.

I am here, aren't I?

Yes.

This is all I can do, Tortula.

It is the first time I have heard my name in many, many years. The sound blows through me like a breath. My body unfurls, opens.

Fine, I say. *But I want you to know—I love you.*

Please, they say, *stop talking.*

46

We move very slowly now. The way is difficult and we are weak. Sometimes the cool, damp air feels like waves pushing us back. Perhaps we will grow gills. I'm saying this and something more when I stop. I feel dizzy, like I might fall.

Something's happening to my brain, I say. *I'm not thinking right.*

Sit for a moment, L says.

I'm not. . . I try to locate the words. *Thinking in straight lines*, I finally say.

I know the feeling you're describing.

The feeling is real.

Yes, the feeling is real, but it's not what is. It's not fact.

It is a fact that I feel, I say, lost, immediately regretting that I decided to try talking at all. L always has enough energy to argue.

Fine, they say. *But your feelings do not create the world. The world is what it is and how you feel about it has little consequence. Now, if your feelings drive thought and that thought drives action, that's a different conversation. But what I want to say now is that your brain is trying to take care of you. Do not fight it.*

47

Sometimes it feels like I've made you up, I say.

Walk, L says.

I move my leg and my foot follows. I can hear L next to me. We are in rhythm with each other's steps.

Perhaps I invented you as the reason I needed to go outside.

L stops. I fall against them and they hold me away. *This is what you think?* they say. *That I don't exist?*

I think many things, I say. I can feel a type of pulsing in the earth—the sea from millions of years ago, the limestone.

What happened to us? I say.

I don't remember, says L.

You hurt me, I say.

You hurt me! L snaps back.

I hear them shuffling around in their pack.

I cannot be the person you want me to be, they say. They find my hand and put a few dried berries in it.

I am sorry, I say.

I am real, they say.

The more L insists, the more I doubt them.

I chew on the berries. Almost too intense. My head is throbbing. I think our path is sloping up. The air pressure changes. We yawn to make our ears pop.

I miss driving, I say, knowing that L will not like it. *I miss sunshine.*

I can hear the click-scratch of L rolling stones over in their palm. I'm amazed that they've held onto them.

You think I'm holding on too tight, I say to L.

Yes, they say.

Their voice is a whisper. It reminds me of a dandelion, orb of white seeds. If I pluck it, the seeds will fly away like tiny feathers.

I don't think you hold on tight enough.

48

There are moments when the mountain sleeps. I do not hear the rustling or the humming, not as much. It slows me in a way that feels kind, full of care. A welcome hollow. The silence is not true silence—I'm not sure there is such a thing—but instead a deep, low, breezy-wet sound, like how I imagine the womb sounds from inside. This reminds me of the baby. Was the baby lost? No, the baby died. What was his name? His name was Ira.

We move together, we sit still. We found each other, but somehow lost our connection.

My chest fills with sadness at the thought.

When I think I cannot go on, I feel the moss stitching the skin of my forehead together. It reminds me of what we could be.

49

There's something you should know, Mother, something I've been too afraid to tell you—

Cyparissus took his own life.

I'm sorry.

Let me start over.

It was a Tuesday. There had been another invasion, and all the firestorms just outside the city had had us in lockdown for months. Cy and I were living together, but at separate ends of the house. We moved through hallways, speechless, like ghosts already.

He made his choice. Prearranged it so that I would not be the person to find him. When the brokers arrived to remove his body, I was not surprised. I had foreseen it on the day he returned to us, something in his eyes—a stain. Unnerving. The war had left a concentrated, shocked-shaky stillness in him.

I struggle with getting this right, telling you in the right way—

I was not sad—I'd already done my grieving for him. Dear brother, who left as a person and returned a symbol. No, I was not sad. I was relieved. Relieved that he was at peace. Relieved that the violence in the house was gone.

I can feel the bile rising in me and it makes me realize I am wrong. There is still grief there, buried deep.

TADPOLE Black dot in the center of each orb. Tiny eyes in a glass bowl. A dot eats its way into the wet underworld. Gills. Translucent tail. Dark comet darts in a whoosh. Glands, mouth. Lungs. A horror in the hindquarters.

50

Do we imagine it? Little shards of light breaking through mountain. Can we be so close to the surface? How long has it been since there were day and night?

In this new light, I can see L's face—how they've aged. Their hair is grey and their outer layer of skin has grown loose around their eyes and hands. They have aged, which means I, too, have aged.

There is more water in the cave than I knew. Waterfalls and ponds and tiny tributaries that snake through the rocky floors. A cathedral of stalactites shimmers above us.

I ask L, *Don't you miss your friends, your family? Don't you yearn for the old ways?*

L sighs. *It feels like someone else's life, no longer mine*, they say.

We sang at Mother's memorial, I say. *Deep in the woods, hidden from view. Cy, a couple friends, old neighbors. There weren't many of us.* I close my eyes.

L leans in, listens.

I can feel it, the song in the air.

The insects of the cave are more than just a scuttle. I can see them. They have antennae and bodies and faces that look like tiny skulls. Once I might have been scared, but now seeing anything alive brings me comfort.

There is a voice in me that is untamed, I say. *It circles and circles, then surprise! It escapes.*

Your grieving voice? L asks.

No, I say. *The voice behind the grieving voice. The one that accepts grief.*

The voice behind the voice, they say.

There is the light that flickers in through the cracks and the light that bounces off the waterfalls, throwing itself this way and that, and the light that holds still to a beam. In light, L reminds me of a stream. Liquid, rushing, always finding their way through the rocks and caverns that I think are dead ends. I imagine L in the gone world, in a purple necktie and ripped jeans sitting with a bunch of friends at a cocktail bar, the only one left in the city. They are laughing, full of joy. Ease. I wonder how long it's been since they felt at peace and I wonder if they will ever feel it again.

Part of me envies you, L says. *That you can recall so easily. You have a story that warms you at night. You keep your old friends near, not thinking of how they all changed. How afraid and hateful everyone became.*

It was not their fault, I say. *They were just trying to survive.*

That's what I'm trying to do now. Survive.

But you chose me, I say. *People need people.*

I suppose that is true, they say. *For as long as people remain.*

51

Mother, I miss you. Sometimes I think about emerging on the other side and hugging the first person I see. Will we see people? I long to be embraced. Sometimes I let myself imagine that you're there waiting for me. In my mind, you are always the version of yourself from before you were taken. Back when you had hope and two working lungs.

Cy told me it was peaceful. Your death. He did not let the brokers harvest your body. He had seen firsthand the experiments you would be used for.

I returned too late to apologize, but not too late to witness. I watched as your body burned. Released by fire, into ash. Into air. It was the only way to know, to *really* know, the only way I'd be able to sleep at night. It was worth the risk.

We sang, even though it hurt. We sang and we coughed and we cried and we embraced each other in secret. Inside each death were many, many more deaths, impossible to hold. We opened our throats to the pain and the joy and the regrets. We sang into the air. We placed the stones. It helped us feel whole. It was as if we were not just mourning people, but a past. Letting go, but not forgetting.

TORTULA MURALIS Smallish. Inside cracks.
A cliff's edge. Branch of oak. Fences, stones, logs. A
beetle's back. Repair. And now, forehead. Moist. Wind
gasps. Turbulent flow. Boundary layer. Canopies. Sun,
shade. Root system. Blood, breath. Water vapor. Lush
wefts. Narrow leaves to slow airflow. Webby, netlike,
semiotic. Frond-speak. Repair. Sip in dampness, rot.
A new beat, a thud. Pulse at the tips. Assemblages.
Geometries. Together-breathe. Together-listen. Repair.

52

Cavern leads to tunnel leads to cavity leads to crevice. The way slopes up. The closer it feels we're getting, the narrower our path becomes until we can no longer stand. L hacks away at the stone.

We crawl on our hands and knees, sometimes our elbows and stomachs, adrenaline thudding through our bodies, L leading the way.

I am changing again. Skin fragile, weak, cracked fingernails, and a tinny taste in my mouth, but I feel the moss. I know the green stars are thriving. I'm starting to see that my longing is not really a longing for a thing—a person, a place—but a feeling of connection.

I think about my bones and muscles, how they all work together, a miracle. I listen as my body shifts from loneliness to another feeling which is not as lonely.

The light is gone. We feel for a seam, a fissure, any way forward. No sleep. Palms and knees bleeding. Our lungs. Hurt.

We dig. My body, near L's. Curled up. Inside myself.

Hack. Hack. Hack.

SEED Mouse melon, tributary tomb, grouse depression, tweed calm and creeping, bee balm and kabocha soft inside a death fruiting, ailing tome, dig, bleed, falling stone, an open weed an open chest an open plot for a hope burial.

53

We break through into caverns. Every time, nothing.

Failure adds up. Closes in. I've failed you. I've failed Cy. I've failed L. Everyone. I am an entire species of failure.

L gasps and thrashes with the pickaxe, trying to work their way through. *This isn't right*, they keep saying in their many voices, high-pitched, sharp, all kinds of afraid. Their skin. Leaks. Hisses. The voices grow angry. A bickering family. Mean.

A thudding. Inside. Body. Starving. Hope-sick. Lost.

The earth closes in around us. The darkness is unrelenting.

54

Our packs are too big. We leave them behind. A relief.

Then a sudden realization grips my chest. We might not make it.

I fill myself with the memory of morning sunlight. I draw in the memory like taking in a breath of music. If I go deep enough, I won't get sad or miss it. Go deep enough and there is gratitude for having once lived in that world.

I think about Nana May's house. I sat on the floor. I remember the carpet. I looked out the window.

Snow, she said. *It's snow.*

Icicles lined her rooftop outside. If someone looked through that window they would've seen a room full of women, mostly grand-mothers. The memory is awash with phantoms. You in the mirror, tugging at your cream-colored nylons.

There is no map, I realize. No song that will bring you back to me.

55

There is something so active about anger, so alive. I didn't believe you would die.

And then Cy's voice telling me that you were gone.

And then the rage roiling through my chest.

And then the dumb haze, helping Cy clear out your room.

And then a menthol cough drop from your mouth on the nightstand.

And then the ache, a rumbling ocean of ache.

And then the pressure in my skull.

And then the house tinged with your absence rubbing up against my everyday.

And then, only then, the massive regret, a continent.

And then, now, a slip. A rupture.

A softening.

56

L stops.

You alright? I say.

Their body emits a long, sharp cry. Piercing, mournful. Worms and beetles swarm. It is unlike any sound I've ever heard, somewhere between wail and song. It makes the mountain walls shiver.

Hey! I reach out.

I wait as their cry dissolves into a weep. L reaches their hand back, grabs mine. Our fingers tangle together.

I feel movement, sprouting, an urgent tug between my eyes. I work my way through our tunnel. Earthworm. I am pressed against L. Their tattered rope of a body.

We have to go up, I say. I take the pickaxe.

I am not sure where in my body I find it, the strength. It is there, though, sudden and multiplying.

I dig and hack into the rock above, this boulder sky which is not really a sky but many layers of earth, full of histories, of creatures, both dead and alive. I sweat what is left of me into the mountain. Dirt falls into my eyes, but my head is clear. I sift the earth, take sips of air. I hack and hack. I pull L behind me.

I break into light.

BULLFROG A lull on the silty edge of the pond. Absorbs air through skin, then slips into a cool wet stillness. Waits. Gills disappearing. Pain, legs, lungs. Swims, sits. Sees forward, sideways, upward. All at once. A singing behind new ears.

57

I pull myself up and out of the earth. I brace myself against the edge of the hole I've made, and reach back for L's hand. I pull them from our grave.

We lie side by side. Two bodies laid out on the mossy ground.

We stare up into a canopy of leaves. The pickaxe—the vehicle—is gone. The air is clean and warm.

Together, we sleep.

58

L and I are deep in the dew-lit green. Ivy twists around the cinnamon sap of a hemlock. Snails slink over wet pebbles.

It is so quiet, I say.

Yes, L says. They point into the overstory. *No birds.*

Can we grow here?

No, we cannot.

We sit with this.

Finally, I stand and pick blackberries from a bush. Hand some to L.

Together, we eat.

Afterward, Lamellae kisses the back of my berry-stained hand. *Alright,* they say. *We'll keep going and we'll forage along the way.*

L pulls the last seeds from their pocket. *Will you teach me the ritual you learned? For letting go?*

Do you still have the stones? I say.

STONE Black with grey speckles like ash in night or tiny abandoned galaxies. Kidney-shaped. Small as a sparrow's egg, but heavy. All the way through. Once volcano, now made smooth by waves. A baby bundled and left on the ocean floor.

STONE The color of red clay. A strange gift. Desert mountain. Wind-smoothed. A dead creature, cool to the touch. Still. Silent. Lumpen and triangular. The size of a duck heart.

STONE Bumpy as a knuckle. Grey speckled with fragments of fossilized shell. Feathered seed pods. A concrete river. Inside—dreams, fears.

59

I thought I could die alone, inside and at peace. Then, The Driver appeared on my doorstep and handed me the last kabocha—humble and sweet and alive in my hands. Now, L shows me the secret lifebreath of water and wind. For them, I make inner landscapes, caverns of thoughts within feelings. I wanted to share it all with you, Mother. I apologize for the blur. It is all I could recover—a postcard watercolor, a whisper.

Here is what remains unsaid: thank you for giving your life to me. You raised me through suffering and so much death. But still, every day, in all manner and suggestion, in your lists and your lessons, with each half-made plan, still, you looked at me as an end in itself, and you said—*live.* Live.

Our discoveries are fleeting, paper-thin—they will not be remembered like this. But maybe by moss, by water running down the stone walls inside of mountains, maybe in gypsum on the bottom of oceans that are gone and the ones that will come after, wave upon wave of chalk dust. And in the landscapes of our minds—our overactive, oversensitive minds, that will continue to interfere with all that is necessary for our survival. So be it. We know no other way.

When all is said and done, let the wind and water continue to transform the earth without us.

Let us be but a breath.

NOTES

5, 38-39: Quotations in these sections are from Anne Carson's "A Lecture on Corners," The Graduate Center, CUNY, 11 July 2018.

40-41: Quotations from unpublished poems written by my great-grandmother, Maya Brodell, 1920-1966.

41: Quotations from a 1968 radio interview with Dolores Huerta.

48-49: "The Slumber Boat" (later known as "The American Cradle Song"), was a lullaby written by Alice Riley and Jesse L. Smith Gaynor, published in 1898.

63-64: Quotations in this section are from "No Place for Self-Pity, No Room for Fear," by Toni Morrison, *The Nation*, 23 March 2015.

79-80: Quotations in this section are from Winona LaDuke's "We Have to Fight," Ottawa, 2012.

ACKNOWLEDGMENTS

EARTH I am grateful for my family. Thank you, Mom, for seeing the creativity in me and for nurturing it. For setting out stamps and scissors and paper on the table, building me a little office under the stairs, helping me create a neighborhood newsletter, coming to my poetry readings, and for listening to the words even when it was hard. Thank you Mike, Mimi, Grampy, Ken, Debbie, and Denny for your love and support. To my brother, Ben, and my cousins Angie, Tim, and Steven for listening to my ghost stories every summer, and to Christina, Vance, Peg, and Carl. To Ellen, who was so sure I would publish a book one day. To Susan and Arlo: come visit again, soon! To Cora, Arthur, and Vivian for their constant comfort. Ever grateful for my loving and supportive partner, Will, who encourages my work, but also reminds me when to eat and when to rest. Thank you all for providing consistent stability, connection, and grounding in this chaotic world.

FIRE I am grateful for friends, teachers, and mentors. Thank you Susan, Nikki, Heidi, Heather, Sam, Gully, Jack, Abby, Davey, Scott, Joseph, Marlys, Tak, Angela, Suzy, and the wonderful Sarah Rose for helping me survive my teens and twenties. To my dear friends Monica, Johann, Sean, Neal, Skylark, Dylan, Anna, Rachel, Adam, Diana, Maree, David, Andrice, Emily, and Lark for their kindness and care. Thank you to my early mentors who lit the flame: Carol Seim, Carolyn Kizer, Kimberly Pollack, Bill Ransom, Sandra Yannone, and Jose Gomez, and to teachers that stoked the fire: Valerie Miner, Pete Fromm, Bonnie Jo Campbell, Alastair Hunt, and Natalie Serber. To David Long for his kind letters and meticulous notes. Thanks to all the editors of the literary journals where I published early work, especially Marisa Siegel and Chelsea Leu at *The Rumpus*, Colleen Burner and Lauren Perez at *Shirley*, Anna Zumbahlen at *Carve*, John Madera at *Big Other*, Raki Kopernik at *Mayday*, and Thea Prieto at *The Gravity of the Thing*. To my Chemeketa colleagues Laura Scott, Amanda Knopf, and Michele Burke. A heartfelt thanks to my writer friends who continue to inspire me: Hannah Pass, Chrys Tobey, Tom DeBeauchamp, Brandi Katherine Herrera, Jessica Henkle, Laura Moulton, Neva Cavataio, Aaron Kier, Jessica Wadleigh, Susan DeFreitas, and Noah Zimmerman. Many thanks to Sabrina Orah Mark and the participants in the Escape & Captivity workshop, all of whom read and encouraged me to keep going with *Sift* in its early stages, and to Azareen van Der Vliet Oloomi and the Lighthouse workshop participants who offered careful feedback and kind words on early chapters.

WATER Gratitude to those who were there for me through the many transformations of *Sift*. Thank you Lucie Bonvalet, TJ Acena, and Dawn Raffel for your thoughtful notes. Thanks to all The 3rd Thing artists, especially Jennifer Calkins, M Freeman, and Diane Exavier. I love, love, love your books. A future thanks to the 2023 cohort—I'm already seeing our rivers merge and the confluence is thrilling. Thank you, Alison, for seeing *Sift*'s potential and for championing it with your whole heart. For your letters and handwritten edits. To those who wrote blurbs and to Heather at Mind the Bird Media, thank you. I am deeply grateful for my therapists, Jennifer and Brenda. Thank you all for braving these rapids with me.

I am profoundly lucky to have found two very special readers along this journey—one who saw the potential in the mess and another who breathed new life into what I thought was finished. I will start with the latter.

AIR I think the best editor is not only someone who sees how a piece can be stronger, sharper, clearer, but also spends the time necessary to take the writer there with her. She is someone who can sift through the clutter and pull out meaning that even the writer might not see. She makes the piece stronger and the artist wiser. She helps the writer see patterns in their work—what to lean into and what to watch out for. To do this well takes a truly gifted individual. Anne, thank you deeply for the care you give artists and their work. For managing to be all the things: patient, compassionate, technically minded, frustratingly logical, and radically, passionately inventive. The ethos of The 3rd Thing and all that you have cultivated is truly a breath of fresh air in the world of publishing. I had in my mind that the relationship between editor and writer that I once dreamed of having, one that consisted of long conversations about art and life, was a relationship that only lived in the past. Thank you for proving me wrong.

Now, the former. The one who saw potential in the mess.

AIR A story is not a story until it finds someone who will lean in, listen. I feel extremely fortunate to have had that early on with *Sift*. Above all else, this book would not have been possible if it weren't for my dear friend and writing ally Tai Woodville. During the early months of the pandemic, we would meet outside on her porch to exchange chapters of our novels. Without her careful read and push to keep going, *Sift* would not exist. I am forever and ever grateful for your enduring support, Tai, for your enthusiastic generosity, and our mind-meld friendship. Thank you for seeing *Sift* so clearly so early on.

AIR And now, thank you, reader, for being a part of the story too.

THE 2023 COHORT

Barbara Earl Thomas | 2023 Cover Artist
Pulling from mythology and history, artist Barbara Earl Thomas creates a contemporary visual narrative that challenges the stories we tell as Americans about who we are. Known for her prints, papercuts, writing and large-scale installations, Thomas's work is included in private and public collections.

Abigail Chabitnoy | 2023 Land Acknowledgment Writer
The poems that appear as part of a land acknowledgment in each 2023 project are excerpts from Indigenous poet Abigail Chabitnoy's ongoing work "DISQUIET ARK."

Summer J. Hart | BOOMHOUSE | Poetry
The poems of *Boomhouse* time-travel the rivers and lakes of the Penobscot and St. John's watersheds from New Brunswick to the Gulf of Maine, navigating spruce covered islands, mill towns, logging camps, family lore, superstition, and the ghost-currents of the author's mixed Native/settler history.

Alissa Hattman | SIFT | Fiction
Two women set out through the haze of social and environmental collapse in search of fertile soil. They travel deserts, burned-over forests, lightless mountain caverns and the terrain of their evolving connection. An invocation, an elegy, a postcard home, *Sift* is about family wounds, humanity's failures, how to care for one another at the end, and how to make a new beginning.

Jean Toomer | CANE: A NEW CRITICAL EDITION, Edited by Diane Exavier, Carlos Sirah & Anne de Marcken | Fiction / Critical Thinking / Oracle
In celebration of *Cane*'s 100th anniversary, Black thinkers and makers have assembled to propose, speculate and imagine our place in the cosmology of Jean Toomer's canefield. Their insights, prompts, gestures and questions are offered with the novel in a deck of oracular cards and companion booklet. Each card is an invitation to readers to respond to *Cane*'s call.

GOOD SYMPTOM: A SERIAL ANTHOLOGY OF TIME-BASED DISTURBANCES
Curated by M Freeman, Rana San & Chelsea Werner-Jatzke | Literary Media Art
Released in 12 monthly installments, this suite of short films troubles the boundaries between literature and cinema. *Good Symptom* showcases experiments that push poetry and flash fiction, manifesto and memoir off the page and onto the screen. Each installment is presented to subscribers with curatorial insights probing the qualities and quirks of this emergent form.

"The third thing" is the idea that emerges when we use imagination instead of compromise to solve a problem, meet a need, repair an injury, right a wrong, answer a question, question an answer, to get where we're going, to go somewhere new.

The 3rd Thing is an independent press dedicated to publishing necessary alternatives. Every year or so we publish a cohort of projects representing in form, content and perspective our interdisciplinary, intersectional priorities. We think of each project in the cohort as a break in the stockade—a way out of the settlement and into the wilderness. Come through.

the3rdthing.press